THE FROG AND THE PRINCESS
and the Prince and the Mole
and the Frog and the Mole
and the Princess and the Prince
and the Mole and the Princess
and the Frog and the Prince
and the Princess and the Prince
and the Frog and the Mole

WRITTEN BY   ILLUSTRATED BY

John Bear & Charlie Powell

TRICYCLE PRESS
Berkeley, California

TRICYCLE PRESS
P.O. Box 7123
Berkeley, California 94707

Cover and text design by Nancy Austin

Library of Congress Cataloging-in-Publication Data

Bear, John B.
      The frog and the princess and prince and the mole / John B. Bear ;
illustrations by Charlie Powell.
            p. cm.
      Summary: A rhyming story of a frog who is returned to his origi-
nal princely form when kissed by a princess, who in turn is transformed
into a mole. Book can be read in both directions.
      ISBN 1-883672-07-4
      1. Upside-down books—Specimens. [1. Fairy tales. 2. Upside-
down books. 3. Toy and moveable books. 4. Stories in rhyme.]
PZ8.3.B375Fr   1994
[E]--dc20   94-2802
                                                                       CIP
                                                                        AC

First Tricycle Press printing, 1994

Manufactured in Singapore

1 2 3 4 5 6 – 97 96 95 94

The frog comes to the princess sweet,
A story sad has he.
He looks at her with mournful eyes,
A frog so sad, the princess cries,
"Please tell your tale to me."

The frog hops in the royal lap
And starts to bare his soul:
"A handsome prince I once was, Miss.
An evil witch has made me this,
For once I kissed a mole."

"Is there no way to end this curse?"
  The princess asks, in pain.
"Ah, yes," says Frog. "Ah, yes," says he.
  "The kiss of one as sweet as thee
  Will bring me back again."

"I really shouldn't," the princess sighs,
While kissing Frog's green head.
She sets him gently on the floor—

A lightning flash! A thunder roar!

A prince is there instead!

The prince bows low and, grateful, says,
"I thank thee, gracious soul."
He stands to see his lady fair,

But lo! the princess is not there,
And in her place, a mole.

The mole comes to the handsome prince,
A story sad has she.
She looks at him with mournful eyes,
A mole so sad, the fellow cries,
"Please tell your tale to me."

The mole crawls in the royal lap,
   As gentle as a dog.
"A lovely princess once I was,
   A witch has made me this because
   One day I kissed a frog."

"Is there no way to end this curse?"
 The prince then asks, in pain.
"Ah, yes," says Mole. "Ah, yes," says she.
 "The kiss of one as fair as thee
 Will bring me back again."

"I really shouldn't," the prince replies,
But kisses Mole's brown head.
He sets her gently on the floor—

A lightning flash! A thunder roar!

A princess there instead!

The princess curtseys low and says,
    Her manner yet agog,
"I thank thee, Sir, for what you've done."
    But lo! the handsome prince is gone,
    And in his place, a frog.

Now *you*, dear Reader, have a choice
    As you are halfway done.
To learn of Frog's uncertain fate,
    And that of Princess, do not wait,
    Return *now* to page one.

But if of Prince and also Mole
    You wish a different look,
Rotate this page around halfway
    And *then* turn back, you know the way—
    A new start to the book!

Now *you*, dear Reader, have a choice
  As you are halfway done.
To learn what happens next to Mole
  And also Prince, if that's your goal,
  Return *now* to page one.

But if of Princess and of Frog
  You wish a different look,
Rotate this page around halfway
  And *then* turn back, you know the way—
  A new start to the book!

The prince bows low and, grateful, says,
"I thank thee, gracious soul."
He stands to see his lady fair,

But lo! the princess is not there,
And in her place, a mole.

A prince is there instead!

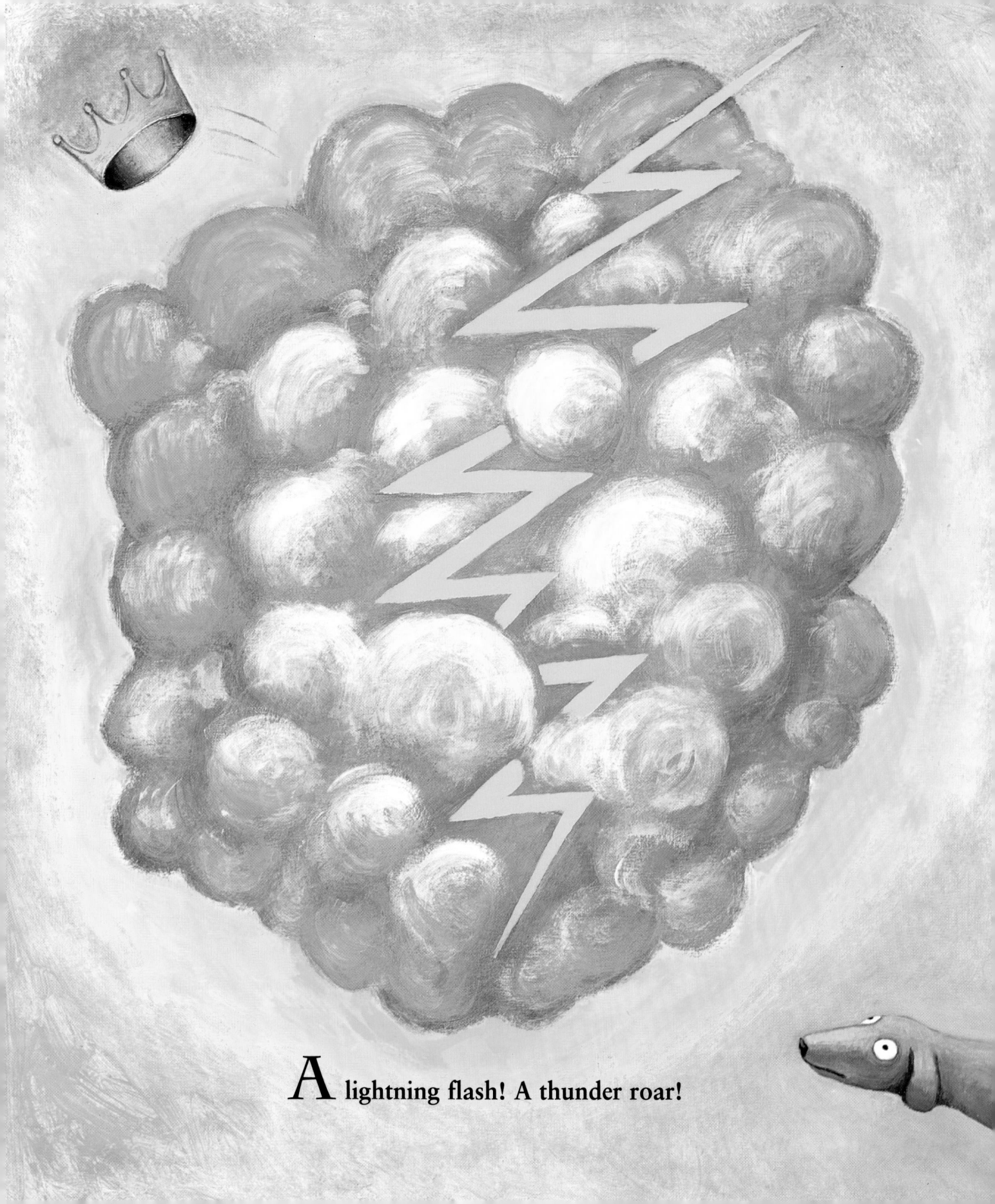

A lightning flash! A thunder roar!

"I really shouldn't," the princess sighs,
While kissing Frog's green head.
She sets him gently on the floor—

"Is there no way to end this curse?"
    The princess asks, in pain.
"Ah, yes," says Frog. "Ah, yes," says he.
    "The kiss of one as sweet as thee
    Will bring me back again."

The frog hops in the royal lap
    And starts to bare his soul:
"A handsome prince I once was, Miss.
    An evil witch has made me this,
    For once I kissed a mole."

The frog hops in the royal lap
And starts to bare his soul:
"A handsome prince I once was, Miss.
An evil witch has made me this,
For once I kissed a mole."

The frog comes to the princess sweet,
   A story sad has he.
He looks at her with mournful eyes,
   A frog so sad, the princess cries,
     "Please tell your tale to me."

The princess curtseys low and says,
    Her manner yet agog,
"I thank thee, Sir, for what you've done."
    But lo! the handsome prince is gone,
    And in his place, a frog.

A princess there instead!

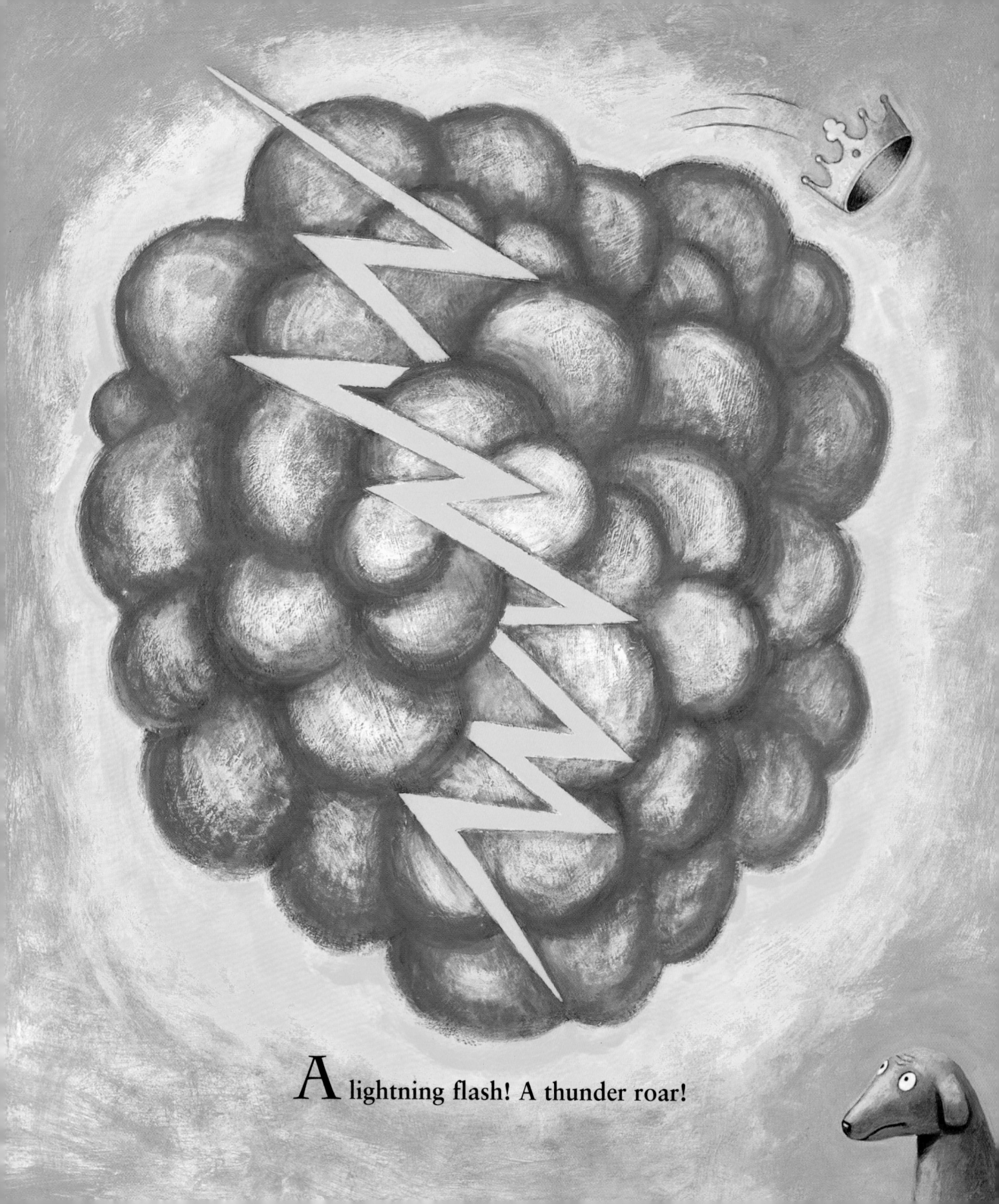

A lightning flash! A thunder roar!

"I really shouldn't," the prince replies,
But kisses Mole's brown head.
He sets her gently on the floor—

"Is there no way to end this curse?"
The prince then asks, in pain.
"Ah, yes," says Mole. "Ah, yes," says she.
"The kiss of one as fair as thee
Will bring me back again."

The mole crawls in the royal lap,
    As gentle as a dog.
"A lovely princess once I was,
    A witch has made me this because
    One day I kissed a frog."

The mole comes to the handsome prince,
   A story sad has she.
She looks at him with mournful eyes,
   A mole so sad, the fellow cries,
   "Please tell your tale to me."

TRICYCLE PRESS
P.O. Box 7123
Berkeley, California 94707

Cover and text design by Nancy Austin

Library of Congress Cataloging-in-Publication Data

Bear, John B.
      The frog and the princess and prince and the mole / John B. Bear ;
illustrations by Charlie Powell.
            p. cm.
      Summary: A rhyming story of a frog who is returned to his origi-
nal princely form when kissed by a princess, who in turn is transformed
into a mole. Book can be read in both directions.
      ISBN 1-883672-07-4
      1. Upside-down books—Specimens. [1. Fairy tales. 2. Upside-
down books. 3. Toy and moveable books. 4. Stories in rhyme.]
PZ8.3.B375Fr 1994
[E]--dc20   94-2802
                                                                              CIP
                                                                               AC

First Tricycle Press printing, 1994

Manufactured in Singapore

1 2 3 4 5 6 – 97 96 95 94

THE FROG AND THE PRINCESS
and the Prince and the Mole
and the Frog and the Mole
and the Princess and the Prince
and the Mole and the Princess
and the Frog and the Prince

and the Princess and the Prince

and the Frog and the Mole

WRITTEN BY   ILLUSTRATED BY

John Bear & Charlie Powell

TRICYCLE PRESS
Berkeley, California